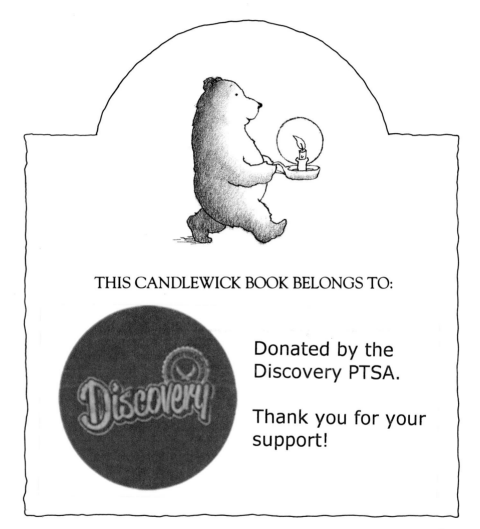

THIS CANDLEWICK BOOK BELONGS TO:

Donated by the
Discovery PTSA.

Thank you for your
support!

**For the Yoo-hoo Girls,
for all the times
we're stuck in the
muck together
P. R.**

**For Tim
J. C.**

Text copyright © 1998 by Phyllis Root
Illustrations copyright © 1998 by Jane Chapman

All rights reserved. No part of this book
may be reproduced, transmitted, or stored in an
information retrieval system in any form or
by any means, graphic, electronic, or mechanical,
including photocopying, taping, and recording, without
prior written permission from the publisher.

First U.S. paperback edition 2003

The Library of Congress has cataloged the hardcover edition as follows:

Root, Phyllis.
One duck stuck / Phyllis Root ;
illustrated by Jane Chapman. — 1st U.S. ed.
p.   cm.
Summary: In this counting book, increasingly larger groups of
animals try to help a duck that is stuck in the sleepy, slimy marsh.
ISBN 978-0-7636-0334-2 (hardcover)
[1. Ducks — Fiction. 2. Marsh animals — Fiction. 3. Counting.
4. Stories in rhyme.]   I. Chapman, Jane, date, ill. II. Title.
PZ8.3.R667On 1998
[F] — dc21   97-34103

ISBN 978-0-7636-1566-6 (paperback)

14 15 16 SCP 22 21 20 19 18 17

Printed in Humen, Dongguan, China

This book was typeset in Myriad Tilt Bold.
The illustrations were done in gouache.

Candlewick Press
99 Dover Street
Somerville, Massachusetts 02144

visit us at www.candlewick.com

One Duck Stuck

Phyllis Root illustrated by Jane Chapman

CANDLEWICK PRESS

Down by the marsh,
by the sleepy,
slimy marsh,

1

one duck
gets stuck in the muck,
down by the
deep green marsh.

Help!
Help!

Who
can
help?

We can! We can!

2

Two fish,
tails going swish,
swim to the duck.

Splish, splish.

No luck.
The duck stays stuck
deep in the muck
down by the
squishy, fishy marsh.

Help!
Help!

Who
can
help?

We can! We can!

3

Three moose
munching on spruce
plod to the duck.

Clomp, clomp.

No luck.
The duck stays stuck
deep in the muck
down by the
swampy, chompy marsh.

We can! We can!

4 Four crickets
chirping in the thickets
leap to the duck.

Pleep, pleep.

No luck.
The duck stays stuck
deep in the muck
down by the
pricky, sticky marsh.

We can! We can!

5

Five frogs
hopping on logs
jump to the duck.

Plop, plop.

No luck.
The duck stays stuck
deep in the muck
down by the
creaky, croaky marsh.

**Help!
Help!**

**Who
can
help?**

We can! We can!

6

Six skunks
climbing over trunks
crawl to the duck.

Plunk, plunk.

No luck.
The duck stays stuck
deep in the muck
down by the
soggy, loggy marsh.

Help!
Help!

Who
can
help?

We can! We can!

7

Seven snails
making slippery trails
slide to the duck.

Sloosh, sloosh.

No luck.
The duck stays stuck
deep in the muck
down by the
slippy, sloppy marsh.

Help!
Help!

Who
can
help?

We can! We can!

8

Eight possums
nibbling on blossoms
crawl to the duck.

Slosh, slosh.

No luck.
The duck stays stuck
deep in the muck
down by the
reedy, weedy marsh.

Help!
Help!

Who
can
help?

We can! We can!

9 Nine snakes
leaving little wakes
slither to the duck.

Slink, slink.

No luck.
The duck stays stuck
deep in the muck
down by the
messy, mossy marsh.

We can! We can!

10

Ten dragonflies
zooming through the skies
whir to the duck.

Zing, zing.

No luck.
The duck stays stuck
deep in the muck
down by the
muggy, buggy marsh.

Help!
Help!

Who
can
help?

We can!

We can!

splish

clomp

pleep

plop

lunk

sloosh

slosh

slink

zing

They
all
help
the
duck
who
got
stuck
in
the
muck.

Spluck!

"Thanks!"
said the duck
who got out
of the muck

down

by the

deep

green

marsh.

PHYLLIS ROOT has written many children's books, including *Oliver Finds His Way*, illustrated by Christopher Denise; *Big Momma Makes the World*, illustrated by Helen Oxenbury; *Rattletrap Car*, illustrated by Jill Barton; and *Kiss the Cow!*, illustrated by Will Hillenbrand. She says she wanted *One Duck Stuck* to be "a north woods wetlands counting book, accurate to the marshes of Minnesota. All the animals are actually found there. I love to go canoeing and camping, and this book is a composite of my experiences." Phyllis Root lives in Minnesota.

JANE CHAPMAN does all her painting in her kitchen, looking out onto the garden. "The color blue in *One Duck Stuck* is the exact same blue that's in my kitchen," she says. Although she has a pet tortoise named Muggs, who at over seventy years old is a family heirloom, one day she would like to have a duck as well. Jane Chapman is the illustrator of *The Emperor's Egg* by Martin Jenkins, *One Tiny Turtle* by Nicola Davies, and *The Story of Christmas* by Vivian French.